A HOUSE OF
BLACK ROBES

A HOUSE OF BLACK ROBES

LANCE CHRISTIAN

authorHOUSE®

AuthorHouse™
1663 Liberty Drive
Bloomington, IN 47403
www.authorhouse.com
Phone: 1-800-839-8640

Published by AuthorHouse   06/19/2012

ISBN: 978-1-4772-2403-8 (sc)
ISBN: 978-1-4772-2402-1 (e)

Library of Congress Control Number: 2012910950

I was among a group of people in front of a large carnival attraction. A decreped old house loomed before us from afar, and I realized that this was another "ghost haunting gimmick." Two workers stood at the entrance and advertised for our patronage as they invited us to "step right up."

While others obliged the men, I did not. In fact, I insisted to myself that I soon turn away. However when I was about to do so, I recognized some of the previous customers that came running back in terror. They did not even begin to take the full tour, but instead had been traumatized from the first few sights they caught a glimpse of.

Upon further inspection of the "haunted house", I recognized certain features of the attraction. I knew of the familiar illusions and parlor tricks. I knew of the secrets and what suprises awaited their unfortunate discoverer. I knew of the demons and the legends tied to them. Suddenly, my fear rapidly decreased and I felt a sense of enjoyment in anticipation to stroll through the darkness I assumed to know. Obligation also weighed itself upon me as I felt I should guide and "protect" the ones I knew.

I walked up to the group who had just made what would appear to be an escape from death. Although I cannot recall what words were spoken, I know that we all ended up heading toward the house. Now the house (although mansion would be a more appropriate term) stood high upon a hill that intimidated all who approached it's path. At the time nothing struck me as extraordinary; I saw everything in order as I would observe any other day. The typical sights and sounds of this attraction, the rides, the blaring music, the flashing lights;all was as one would expect it to be.

However halfway up the hill, a most peculiar event had occured. Everything around me had changed to an old, outdated fashion. Billboards and the words written upon them took on the look of the early 1900s. The ground once paved with black top was replaced with long overgrown grass and countless weeds. But the most unusual of all, was that everything I saw was now in shades of gold and brown as if viewed in an old silent movie.

It was then that I realized I had made a grave error and that this was no attraction of any sort. I tried to escape, but I could not even muster the strength to turn around. It was as though some unseen force would not allow me to leave until I saw everthing that was meant to be seen. Yet as the moments began to pass, I felt that understanding the true nature of this place would not necessarily guarantee me an exit.

As I looked at the people I recognized from the begining (perhaps for a type of desperate comfort) I experienced a grim revelation that robbed me of any hope. Their appearance began to fade away and alter until they became complete strangers. The looks on their faces were ones of saddness and guilt; they knew that they had tricked me. It was the only way that they could get me to accompany them; by taking on the forms of my family and friends. But who were these people, and why did they need me to begin with? As I was gathering all of this information, I realized we were no longer walking, but floating. All of us were automatically guided up the hill as if on an escelator.

When we reached the top of the hill, we were met with a small stone pathway that lead into a courtyard. At that moment, another transformation took place. The clothes that everyone was wearing became bright and highlighted with color, as if exposed under a dark light. But there was another more important appearance. I saw different words and pictures, all of them negative, located on various parts of everyone. The words were written in a language that I had never seen before; yet at the same time, I knew that they were derogatory. These alien words and graphic symbols were the most illuminated. To my horror, I had glanced down at myself and discovered that I now shared the same look.

The courtyard itself was even more unkept than the hill. The grass, although much higher and thicker, had long since dried out. The weeds were now also decorated alongside bristles and thorns. Sections of the earth had now been split open from long neglect and harsh weather, exposing hardened soil and dead roots. The natural debris was also littered with outdated, rusting tools. There were even a few vintage toys that had been tossed about. Of particular note was a rotting, wooden doll next to a tattered baby carriage that had fallen on it's side. A crumbiling, stone birdbath decorated with chipped paint and dried water rings had also shown signs of abandonment.

After passing through this courtyard and surveying the area, I suddenly felt an excruciating pain peirce my head. Wisdom, as if in the form of fire, burned through out my entire skull. Then almost as soon as it started; it disappeared. However, I now knew more than I would have ever had guessed at the carnival site. Perhaps this was the gift of divine insight. Nevertheless, I now began to understand the nature of all of this; where I was, who these people were, and what events would take place.

I was somewhere in the afterlife, and those who acompanied me were the recently departed. Surely this was not Heaven, but could it truely be Hell? Regardless of where I was in the hereafter, there was something noticably wrong. Time itself refused to march forward, and for whatever reason was stuck in a loop. It was as though the fabric of space and time had been wrought with such a terrible ordeal, that it would no longer function until it's wound was healed. But what had happened? That I did not know, and the more I tried to theorize, the more that intense pain returned to my head. I supposed that information was not ready to make itself available to me just yet. I would understand more as I explored this mansion, and perhaps at it's end; the final answer awaited.

Suddenly the earth began to emit a small tremor. I also noticed that the shadows cast from the old tools and toys began to lengthen like a sunset was cast upon them. Not only did the shadows grow in length but they also began to waiver and alter in apperance, completely mismatching their solid counterparts. After a few moments I could now make out the shape of these mysterious shadows; they took on the form of large panthers. These panthers, still painted along the ground in the true nature of a shadow, momentarily surveyed the area. As soon as they caught a glance of myself and the others however, they immediatly began to focus in and charge us. As they ran, they would leap from within the ground and when they were airborn, they solidified and became as real as you or I. The moment they touched the earth though, they once again became shadows fixed into the ground.

Everyone began to scatter in terror as the panthers split off in various directions and lunge at us. Some of the panthers even had the ability to cast themselves alongside the walls of the mansion and leap from the side. The growls that these supernatural beasts made were truely ferocious. They struck terror into my heart each time I heard them roar. As we all ran though, I came to the almost immediate conclusion that these beasts were intentionally holding back. Their purpose was not to destroy us, but to herd us inside of the mansion like cattle. After a few chaotic moments of cat and mouse we managed to head towards the mansion's forboding entrance. A small crowd had formed in front, and as badly as I wanted to escape the shadow panthers, my exit was blocked. Slowly the crowd began to move inside as the panthers began to charge us from behind. Finally the last of the group made it inside and as I pushed myself in, one of the shadow panthers leapt toward me and lashed his claws upon me, tearing my pantleg and leaving a small gash upon my calf.

At that moment, the huge doors slammed shut behind us as I fell to the floor. Out of breath, I laid among the middle of the crowd and was in awe at the sights my eyes beheld. The mansion had to be supernatural itself as it seemed to posess the abilities of being a single living entity. Somehow it was able to manipulate it's shape and appear differently on the inside as opposed to it's exterior. The interior looked nothing like a mansion or any form of living quarters; in fact this area could best be described as a "realm".

The floors stretched out to such a great width that it was impossible to see where they would end. Although I use the term "floors", the ground itself had the appearance of a constant swirling mist. The many different "walls" were nothing more than numerous, black curtains that scarcely seperated the area and formed an abstract maze. These curtains stretched up many feet above and loomed over all of us. However there was no ceiling whatsoever; instead a great night sky filled the area, and in the distance a lunar eclipse faintly illuminated this otherwise dark land.

Suddenly a great gust of wind blew throughout the realm and chilled all of us to the bone. The curtains danced wildly in unison and from the darkness within, I could barely make out some type of sillhoute. Before I could think of what to do, an overpowering light peirced forth from the center of the maze and temporarily blinded us. Once we regained our eyesight, the figure could now be seen in vivid detail . . . and the fact that it's secrecy was now no more, offered little in the way of comfort.

It was a tall, gaunt being in a black robe. At this moment, I could not even tell for certain whether it was human or not. The being also wore a black hood and veiling it's face, was a long white cloth. There were holes cut out of the cloth for it's eyes and mouth; but for some bizarre reason, this being had painted it's face black underneath, giving a very distorted and errie contrast of colors. In it's left hand it held a twisted, medium sized dagger with the blade facing downward. The being stood in a slightly crooked stance.

It soon began to speak in a language that I did not recognize in a tone that was most otherworldly. Suddenly that pain returned to my head and I clenched both of my temples as the feeling was now more intense. Yet as soon as the pain started, it left just as fast. Gradually I was now able to understand what the being was saying, however the sound of it's voice was no less disturbing.

"bEiNgS oF tHiS aPpOiNtEd TiMe, CoMe FoRtH aNd EnTeR iNtO yOuR cHoSeN dEsTiNiEs. FoR hE aWaItS."

The being now stood to the side of the maze's entrance and held a curtain open. With his other arm, now outstretched, he opened his palm toward us and motioned for us to enter. As it did this we were all mystically pulled toward the curtains as if by magic. Single file, we all entered into the dark corridor, with myself being the last in line. As I passed the black robe, I noticed a small silver pendilum around it's neck, underneath it's clothes. As soon as I tried to study the pendilum and identify it, a small centipede crept out from the being's robe and quickly crawled up into it's veil. In revulsion I was taken back, and before I knew it, I now found myself within the darkness of the maze.

Once I entered, the curtain shut and a slight sense of panic ensued as we were now enveloped in complete darkness.

I as well as the others awkwardly walked forward in the blind trying to find some form of direction. Suddenly in the distance there was a faint flicker; the only source of light available. As we all ran toward it's origin, I began to experience a feeling of deja vu. I was almost certain that I knew this place; something about it had tied me too it, though I did not know what. At last, we found the light to be a single torch against a crude stone wall. Oddly enough, the curtains were now no more, but instead replaced with dank stone walls. We then travled to the second light which was another torch. This time the ground was visible and appeared to be a spiral stairway leading downward. The air was humid and stagnant and the ground was damp with stale water. As we descended further, moss began to form in various patches along the walls.

After what seemed to be an eternity, we had reached a large, thick wooden door with a small barred window in the center. The handle was a round iron hoop and resembled a medieval style akin to a dungeon. From within, laughing, almost to the point of hysteria could be heard. On the center of this door was a sheet of bright construction paper that appeared to be pasted on with glue. A single word was written upon the paper in crayon. It filled the entire sheet in big, wildly drawn letters as if scrawled by a child. However I could not read the word as it was written in presumably the same foreign language that the black robe being spoke. Before I could even think to expect it, the same horrendous pain entered into my head; this time gradually begining to enter into the rest of my body. When I looked up at the sign again, the pain began to deminish, and the letters started to form into something different. I now understood what it meant; the word "**MOCKERY**" presented itself before me.

With dread, I used both of my hands to hold onto the door's ring and pull it open. The weight of the door was extremely heavy and took every ounce of strength just to begin to cast it open. After a few overwhelming moments, I had at last succeded. However the laughing was now far louder and in greater volume. It first sounded to come from only a few people, but now it could easily be identified as thousands.

As I ventured further within, I was both shocked and apauled at my discovery.

There were countless crowds of people shackled and chained inside a large, circular room. In the center of the room was a huge tower constructed of giant television sets. The televisions were set up haphazardly and faced all directions, so that every prisoner within this cell could see what was being displayed. The content shown from the numerous televisions was barbaric to say the least. Every violent crime, every sadistic method, every twisted cruelty to disturb mankind was shown in vivid, explicit detail. More shocking than this was the manner of how these prisoners were being treated. As I looked closer at the prisoners, I could see that devices were put upon their faces that kept their eyelids open. The prisoners were laughing so hard that tears streamed down their cheeks in such volume that they became red and chapped.

Before I could investigate anymore, the pain within my body returned, this time feeling as though I was engulfed in white hot fire. My body convulsed as I was temporarily in a state of shock. For a split second, I heard a voice; and I knew it to be from the black robe. All that was spoken was the word, "uNdErStAnD."

Finally the pain left and more of the answers that I was searching for became clear. Though I could not hardly believe it, I was in fact in purgatory. But once again, I felt that something was not right; especially after viewing more of this area. Purgatory was supposed to be a place of cleansing yet . . . was this degree of atonement truely divine?

These prisoners who were laughing so hysterically, were in fact the souls of all those who mocked grave matters. The ones who made jokes at anothers misfortune in life. The ones who blasphemed all things sacred and spit at the face of God. They were the same people whose comments were the most explicit and cruel, hurtful and thoughtless.

Yet they had no form of repentance, reparation or remorse while they lived. They were now forced to see the truth;what exactly it was that they found so humorous. To their horror, they were now each filled with dread and an endless amount of sorrow. However they could only laugh. They laughed hard and were forced to laugh for every second of their time here while constantly viewing these twisted images. The prisoners necks were all red and swollen from lauging so hard and so often; some of the necks had burst open spilling blood and saliva. All of them began to vomit from the intense pain the laughter had caused them. With all of the poison that had spilled forth from their mouths in life, it now seemed only fitting that they be covered in their own vomit in death.

How badly they each wanted to leave this place! How sorry they each were now that they were exposed to the same evil that they had spread in life! But there would be no comfort for these souls. They would only laugh as hard as they wanted to wail in torment.

Suddenly I heard intense screaming from behind me. As I turned around, I saw that new shackles and chains sprung forth from the floor. They latched out and attatched themselves to some of the people I was traveling with. The symbols upon their bodies started to glow a crimson red; it represented that this was in fact the crime that they were guilty of. This was the realm where some of them would now be forced to carry out their sentence. The widening of their eyes and the realization of horror upon their faces was the most genuine form or terror I had ever borne witness to.

Before I could even do anything, a great, steel door appeared before myself and the rest of the travelers. A large pillar of fire materialized next to it reaching high towards the heavens, and then sinking into the ground. Once the fire went out, a great deal of smoke filled the area choking everyone in the room. Once the smoke had dissipated, another black robe stood before us.

This being had the same black robe and hood as the first, however this one wore a mask of silver. The silver mask was in the shape of a large flame. There were no holes for it's eyes or nose, but the mask had been cut off at the point of the being's jaws, allowing it speech. In it's right hand the being held a silver chalice decorated in the same manner as the mask. The content within the chalice seemed to be acidic and possesed a strong smell that made my eyes water. The being began to speak:

"tHe FiRsT aCt Of JuStIcE hAs BeEn CoMmItTeD! cOnTiNuE oNwArD. FoR hE aWaItS."

The black robe waved his arms, and at once the steel door creaked open. Once again we were all drawn inside, in the same manner, by the same force. As I looked back to the travelers we would leave behind, I noticed that their screams began to turn into the same laughter as their new brethern.

Again, I was the last in line and as I passed the black robe, I noticed another small silver pendilum around the beings neck. I found more detail than the first being's pendilum but was still unable to make it out. Again, I desperately tried to study the pendilum, but as soon as I did, this black robe filled my heart with an intense sorrow and distracted my observation. The steel door slammed shut behind me, and once again I found myself in a new relam.

The next area we entered into was most unexpected. It was a long straight hallway filled with the most elegant artwork and high class fashion. Beautiful sculptures were set alongside, as the most awe inspiring paintings decorated the walls. The carpet that we walked upon was priceless in value as it was both exotic and intricatly detailed. Vases crafted by the most skilled artists sat upon fine marble tables imported from various parts of the world. The walls were painted with such superb quality, that the amount of time taken to complete such a task would appear to be eternal. Crystal chandeliers hung from above and had shown the light in a most heavenly manner.

After taking in all of the glamourous sights, we had at last reached the end of the hallway. An enormous, double sided door made of pure gold stood before us. Within the center of the golden door was another word in the same nature as the first realm. However this time the word was made entirely of diamonds and crafted into the door with platinum. The word read "PROFIT."

Oddly enough, I was able to open the door with great ease, but when I stepped inside, I was met with another contradicton. Expecting to enter into a great palace, I instead found myself in the center of an old, run down diner. The booths were covered in dust and cobwebs, while the floor was coated with a thick, brown grime. All of the patrons of this diner appeared to be fastened to their chairs. They all ate hesitantly as if they were already full; yet their plates were loaded with food.

When I looked closer however, I discovered that the details were far more macabre. The food that these patrons were forced to eat, was nothing remotely close to being edible. It was some type of foul smelling, maggot infested, black slime. This disgusting essence seemed to be alive as it bubbled and gurgled whenever the patrons stabbed into it with their dirt covered silverware. As I watched the patrons being forced to eat such waste I had to struggle with my own feelings of becoming ill.

What of this world could possibly be so vile and at the same time fed to man?

I began to walk further into the diner to discover what the nature of this abominable place was all about. As I passed more of the patrons, I discovered that their bodies became more bloated in appearance. Their insides were at the very breaking point of bursting. Between that agony and being forced to constantly consume such a horrendous element, their reality was nothing short of Hell.

In the background, I noticed an old fashioned jukebox. It was covered in even more dust then the booths, and looked as though it remained untouched for eternity. However as soon as my eyes crossed it's path, the jukebox immediatly sprung to life. The needle scratched long and hard for a few moments. Suddenly it's lights flickered and flashed as it began to play a record and blare it's music loudly:

"The best things in life are free But you can get up to the birds and bees I need money—that's what I want—That's what I want"

Suddenly a deep passion burned inside of me and everything became crystal clear. All of the memories of these patrons became one with me and I knew everything about their lives. They all had one thing in common.

"Your love give me such a thrill But your love don't pay my bills I need money—that's what I want—That's what I want"

Sex, drugs, gambling . . . Peddlers of every form of vice now found their home here. All those who lived off of another's addiction.

Politics, power . . . All those who literally sold their souls. Since they traded integrity for gold in the world of men, they would now reap the true benifits of their misdeeds in the afterlife.

That sickening slime that they were forced to eat, was the very essence of evil. Evil in it's most raw form. Evil so pure that it hadn't yet evolved into anything appealing that man would willingly jeopardize his soul over. All of these patrons were the souls of those who chose the ways of a fallen world over any form of virtue. They were more content with their earthly possesions and recogniton from their fellow man . . . regardless of how they came to acquire it.

Just as they lived off of others in the past, so too would they feed off of that same disgusting evil like vultures to a corpse.

I saw countless visions as that damned song played. I saw life being terminated. I saw crooked deals being made.

"Money don't get everything it's true But what it don't then I can't use I need money"

I saw children being corrupted. I saw families being torn apart.

"—that's what I want—"

I saw power being abused. I saw people being exploited.

"That's what I waannnt—That's what I want"

Criminals walked free and the wicked were being rewarded. Looking about the diner, I saw currency from every nation at every period in time scattered about the area. From the American dollar and Japanese yen to the golden doubloon. This sin was truely universal. How many evils we had comitted as a society in the name of wealth.

Though valuable in life, this great deal of currency scattered about in abudance, was completely worthless in death. The very sight of it all tormented the patrons as they realized they had put something so insignificant and temporary before paradise.

The visions in my head were now more severe and the feelings more intense. I saw bodies falling to the ground and people killing themselves. I saw blood and flames and utter destruction. I heard the cries for help and I felt the tears being shed. I knew the despair and the anxiety and the inability to escape from it all. All of the different thoughts; the different lives raced throughout my mind and swelled up inside of me.

The music now began to play louder, almost to the point of being unbareable. Suddenly the jukebox began to spill large amounts of blood as it screamed it's final refrain:

"Money Lots of Money Whole lotta money"

The blood streamed along the floor and covered my shoes, putting me in the middle of a crimson puddle.

At last I screamed at the top of my lungs and the diner began to disappear. I noticed that some of the people I was traveling with began to glow that same red color on various parts of their bodies. They were guilty of this crime and were now being sentenced.

I tried to run out and help them, but as soon as I touched one of them, the entire area was enveloped in a bright light. The light was so intense, that everyone and everything else turned into ash and began to blow away. The diner had now completely vanished; all that was left was myself and half of the travelers. We now stood helpless in this seemingly endless, bright light.

All of a sudden, this bright light formed into a single beam leaving the rest of the area in darkness. From the first beam, another beam was formed and they diagonally crossed eachother back and forth high above. It was then that I understood these two beams to be spotlights.

With that realization, a long, red carpet rolled out towards us. In front of the red carpet stood a row of glass doors. Above the glass doors was a giant marquie with flashing lights. The marquie read **"SELF."** From the center glass door, the third black robe emerged.

As I crossed the red carpet with the rest of the travelers, cameras began to flash and fanfare began to play. I met the third black robe halfway up the red carpet, yet I soon discovered that the nature of this black robe differed from the other two.

This black robe had no hood or mask of any sort, but instead wore a fine bronze knight's helmet. In it's right hand it carried a bronze mace to match; the spikes of the mace being beautiful sapphires. This black robe also seemed to convulse a bit more than the first, and unlike the other two robes, did not directly address us. Instead it only chanted eerily:

"bRoKeN bOnEs AnD sHaTtErEd DrEaMs AnD bRoKeN bOnEs AnD sHaTtErEd DrEaMs AnD . . ."

I had no idea what the third black robe meant, but he seemed obsessed with those words, perhaps even tormented by them. When I looked for this being's pendilum, it flung open the glass doors and a thick mist blew in. At once we were all covered in it's essence and nothing but the mist could be seen. Fading in the background I once again heard the third black robe cry out his refrain:

"bRoKeN bOnEs AnD sHaTtErEd DrEaMs AnD bRoKeN bOnEs AnD sHaTtErEd DrEaMs AnD !!"

At once the words of the third black robe stopped and the mist lifted. Everyone now found themselves in the middle of a thick, wet marsh. Mud and dead leaves were up to our knees, and trying to trek through this mire proved to be most difficult. Countless rotting trees protruded randomly in the background. Though the mist had lifted enough for visibility, the environs were no less dreary.

As we continued to journey onward, not fully knowing what to look for, the mud now reached up to our waists and hindered us even more so. Shockingly enough, when I looked down at the mud, I swore that I saw human faces and the mud caked onto my hips resembled human hands. As the wind blew, I scarcely heard a whisper;

"hOw We WiSh We CoUlD rIsE uP tO tHeIr LeVeL, sO tHaT wE cOuLd DrAg ThEm DoWn To OuRs!"

A faint laughter followed and as I looked up, I saw a great hill of mud before me. At the top of the hill was a grand altar in the shape of the world. On both sides of the altar were the first two black robes. All around the hill I saw the strongest of men, the most intelligent of scholars and the most beautiful of women trying to climb it. They all had tied to their wrists great baskets that carried burdens of gold, perfume, and scrolls. As much as they tried to climb the hill and keep their offerings clean, they fell numerous times and soiled not only their precious gifts, but their own garments as well. As if that were not enough, a pestilence of insects swarmed down upon these condemned.

The few that made it to the top of the hill, tried to justify themselves to the two black robes. But the more they tried to excuse themselves the more handicapped they became in both eloquence and charisma. Until finally they became nothing more than mindless vegtables and fell back into the mud, where they sank to the bottom.

Once more the pain returned inside my head, and more information was granted to me;this riddle could now be solved. This was the land of vanity, where the arrogant would be condemned. These beings who neglected others and thought themselves better than everyone else. And at the height of that arrogance was the atheist; the one who did not need God, and belittled all those who did. The one who thought he had all the answers. The one who belived it was always about himself.

Then the whisper returned to me, "yEsSsS! iN lIfE tHeY wErE sUcEsSfUl At PrEsEnTiNg ThEiR gIfTs To The WoRlD; bUt HoW hIgH wAs ThE cOsT?? hOw MaNy HeArTs WeRe BrOkEn?? HoW mAnY sPiRiTs CrUsHeD?? fOr AlL tHaT tHeY ExCeLlEd In, ThEy LaCkEd EvEn MoRe. ThEsE bEiNgS pOsSeSeD sO MaNy GiFtS, yEt ThEy CoUlD NoT FaThOm ThEiR oRiGiN. sUcH FoOlIsHnEsS gIvEs BiRtH tO tRaGeDy . . ."

As I looked at the hill once more, I could now see the faces in the mud more clearly. I could see the arms pulling the condemned down and dragging them into the moist earth. For a few moments as I surveyed this forsaken quagmire, I could see underneath the mud, the bodies of millions.

The whisper, now a booming voice shouted out in a rage;

"wE ArE tHe ViCtImS oF InJuStIcE! sOnS oF SoRrOw AnD dAuGhTeRs Of DeSpAiR! tHe ReCiPeNtS oF tHeIr AcTiOnS! wE aRe ThE cOmBiNeD hAtErEd Of EvErY vIcTiM! aLl ThOsE hUmIlIaTeD aNd ScOrNeD, fOrSaKen AnD cAsT aSiDe!!"

I understood furthermore what the voice was insinuating.

At long last, the lambs would attack the lions. The servants would reign over the masters. In life these condemned were among the most intelligent, talented and beautiful. Their severe lack of humility however, tainted any of it's worth.

Now even more arms and faces formed from within the mud, not only in the hill but out toward the travlers and myself.

"wE wErE cOnDeMnEd By ThE wOrLd BuT tHe WoRlD iS No MoRe! FoRgIvEnEsS rUnS DrY fOr ThEsE fOoLs! We DeMaNd VeNgEnCe!!"

All but three of the travlers and myself were glowing that blood red color again. The newly condemned were of course guilty of this crime, but I was not nearly prepared for how the punishment would be carried out.

I could do nothing as my body was paralyzed with perhaps the same mystic force as from the begining. But as strange as it may sound, I do not know which fate was worse;being condemned or watching the condemned. All around me I saw men and women slowly being dragged down into oblivion. Some were only inches away from me, just close enough to frantically grab on to me;but I could do nothing to help them. I could only watch the terror on their faces, I could only listen to their screams. The three other innocent travelers were just as disturbed as I was;forced to watch such an act take place.

The mud slowly covered their chest, then up to their face . . . slowly, slowly . . . into their mouths and noses . . . so cruel, so twisted. Why? Why did I have to see this? It was too much. I needed to run away;I just needed to escape . . . leave all of this . . . Finally I blacked out.

The sound of wild cheering and applause could be heard. Then swords clashing, then gunshots. Again more cheering. I frantically jolted myself up as I recalled my past predicament. When I looked around, I saw the three other travelers sitting at various points of a roundroom. They looked at me with concern. Was I out for a long time? Did that really happen? It's just the four of us so . . . my God . . . what other horrors could possibly await? When will this nightmare end?

As I looked about the room, I noticed a large steel portcullis on the opposite end of where I was sitting. It reached all the way up to the ceiling and was about half the width of the room. Above the gate loomed a huge sign made of bone which read **"DEATH"**.

With the loud cheering and the sound of weaponry, I figured this place to be the entrance to a coliseum. I gently touched the portcullis and as I did it began to rise as if beckoning for me and the others to enter. When I removed my hand however, I discovered fresh blood had stained it. What I entered into was a place of fire, steel, ash and blood. Of all the sights I beheld during my journey, this was the most barbaric.

This coliseum was built of numerous steel walls, layered with skin and freezing to the touch. All around the top of the coliseum were numerous blood stained smokestacks that refined body parts into firey ash and then billowed it out into the air. The "audience" within the coliseum, were in fact skinned bodies;legs and arms cut off, impaled on spears protruding from the ground. Though they appeared to be dead, their souls were very much alive and in agony; prisoners in their own husks. Most hideous of all was the ground upon which I walked;for it was impossible to move anywhere without stepping on the corpses of babies.

In the center stage of all this were a frenzied group of people armed with various weapons. They were relentless in their attacks on eachother and had all gone berserk with rage. Littered about the grounds of the coliseum were every kind of weapon known to man. The area on which they stood became more and more saturated with blood as they continued to swing their swords and fire their rifles. Yet death would not come for any of them, and that was their greatest torment;they could no longer kill. They could only butcher one another for eternity.

The cheering grew more fierce as the assaults became more vicous. Blood would spray from the center stage and rain down upon the audience. On ocassion, a fiery portal would open up in the smoke polluted sky and drop dozens of new mortals into this pit. At every occurance, the combatants went wild with bloodthirst as they had fresh flesh to slaughter.

High above the audience, I noticed a small dark chamber which held an emperor's throne inside, though I could not make out who sat upon it. In front of the throne were the first three black robes, plus one more. This new black robe levitated in the air and floated down in front of me.

This black robe wore a sadomaschist leather mask and carried a whip stained with dried blood. When the being spoke to me, the sound of two voices speaking at once emitted:

"Do YoU uNdErStAnD tHe NaTuRe Of ThIs PlAcE? tHe EtErNaL sUfFeRrInG fOr AdVoCaTeS oF eVeRy FoRm Of ViOlEnCe. tHe GlOrY oF tHe SaDiSt. tHe ReWaRd FoR tHe KiLlEr. tHe AbOliShMeNt Of LiFe At EvErY sTaGe. NoThInG mUsT eXiSiT. cOmPlEtE eRaDiCaTiOn.

YeSsSsSsSsSsSsSsSsS . . .

Soon the last three travelers flashed red on various parts of their bodies, but unlike the other condemned, there was no terror, only rage and mania. At once they picked up weapons off of the ground and rushed towards battle in the crowd. They soon bore gashes and lost limbs and laughed hysterically as they joined this unending warfare.

"If YoU pRoCeEd FuRtHeR yOu WiLl UnDeRsTaNd AlL. FoR hE aWalTS. bUt . . . WhY nOt StAy HeRe WiTh Us?"

At once the black robe raised his hand towards a club lying on the ground. The club levitated and flew towards me, and at once it was clenched inside of my fist;I could not let go. Suddenly the fighting of the combatants stopped and they all moved aside. The cheering from the audience had also subsided.

At the back of the coliseum was a single man on the ground sitting against the wall;he was severely wounded. When he looked up at me, I recognized him. He was a man who had seriously wronged me in my life, in fact I would consider him my most bitter enemy.

"bEcAuSe We KnOw OnLy DeAtH, wE sEeK oNlY aNnHiLaTiOn. YoU cAnNoT eDuCaTe ThOsE dEsTiNeD fOr IgNoRaNcE . . ."

"kIlL" the black robe spoke.
"kIlL"
"kIlL"

The force around my hand that clenched the club grew tighter and tighter. The fighters began chanting as well.

"Kill"
"Kill"
"Kill"

Then the audience began screaming those words;

"KILL"
"KILL"
"KILL"

I began to breath in deep the fire and ash of the realm, sweat dripped from my brow as I started to walk up toward my enemy. When I approached him, my mind felt like one great churning ball of fire and electricity seemed to flow through my viens. The power was so great as I held the club over him. Damn him! I wanted to make him pay! I wanted to make him suffer!

I was just about to strke the blow, when he looked up at me and our eyes met. His face beaten and pathetic, his body limp and torn. He began coughing up blood before forcing a couple words from his mouth.

"have . . . mercy" he whimpered.

Suddenly my heart was overwhelmed with saddness, and all of my desire for vengance waned. As if reacting to my emotions, my hand easily loosened it's grip and the club fell to the ground beside my old foe.

At once the fourth black robe shrieked in outrage;

"yOu!! wE cAnNoT uSe YoU!! nOt YeT!! sOoN hOwEvEr, YoU wIlL kNoW yOuR pLaCe!!"

With a wave of it's arms, darkness cast itself all over the entire area. Gradually everything was blacked out in front of me. The very last thing to disappear from my vision was the black robe's pendilum. I only saw it for a second, but I was shocked. Surely it couldn't have been??

I was now in a deep void;an absolute nothingness. No matter where I would run, I would end up in the same place. There was no time, no space;nothing. I was alone in this silent darkness with no hope of escape. It was a type of darkness that could be felt creeping upon your skin. The type of darkness that would choke you every time you breathed.

All of a sudden I heard a deep moaning from behind me, when I turned around to see what it was, I was shocked to see all of the travelers that I had first entered with. However they appeared much different from before;void of any human emotion or thought. The moaning grew louder, and I then discovered legions upon legions of these condemned. They were all walking toward me and suddenly I felt a great sense of unease. What did they want with me? They all started to reach out and grasp at me. All I could do was run in the darkness. Regardless of where I ran, the moaning got louder. They were getting closer and closer until at last I could sense that they were begining to surround me.

At last, some light began to appear and I could now make out a hallway in front of me. Written in blood upon both sides of the walls were the words; "BROKEN BONES AND SHATTERED DREAMS AND BROKEN BONES AND . . ."

As I ran down this errie hallway with the damned lashing at my shadow, I prayed to be graced with an escape. Soon I noticed an exit which had a huge rusty thurible looming above it. The word "GRUDGE" was engraved upon it's surface.

Just then more of the condemned began to appear and it seemed that they would soon overwhelm me. In a last ditch effort for survival, I jumped through the corridor as the doors slammed shut behind me. I could now hear them clawing on the other side;their moaning now muffled.

I was safe for the time being as I had at last arrived to the final chamber in this dimension. It was extremely vast and completely circular in nature, as if entering a large tower.

The walls were made of purple bricks and gave off a dark glow as they illuminated the atmosphere with an aurora of eternal midnight. These walls stretched far up into space, and the stars and planets constantly raced back and forth as they darted along this open portal. It was a scene of unending and unearthly chaos that cursed the heavens as the sky seemed to scream in torment.

The highest reaches of these walls were decorated with weathered disintegration and caked with long since dried blood. These wicked stains had gradually left their orgins and painted itself downward in various deadly streams.

Many pieces within the walls had fallen apart and acted as enormous, primitave windows which displayed the previous levels of this universe: **MOCKERY, PROFIT, SELF and DEATH**.

I realized that the small rivers of ancient blood plastered upon these walls spilt around these windows and danced diagonally and eratically before reaching the bottom;defying gravity.

I could clearly hear the wailing and the begging of mercy; the howls of regret and the cursing of self-hate. I became completely immobile as a sound of torture pierced the air, and a declaration of insanity from a newly broken mind soon followed.

Even greater atrocities were being comitted from the various locations. Observations no mortal should ever be damned to look at. Visions so horrific, I begged God to strike me blind.

With every ounce of my strength I forced myself onward and was even more shocked when my eyes detailed the earth.

The ground on which I stood was completely invisible, and below me was an abyss of darkness which, at it's end, lie a pool of white fire.

As I graudually walked forward, pillars of fire shot up through the darkness and reached for my every footstep, as if alive. Fortunately the thin invisible barrier shielded me from the hungry flames.

Ever cautious, I contiued to venture forward;heart racing, palms sweating. I felt the soles of my feet begin to blister as the enraged inferno became more violent with it's passionate attempts to consume me.

Hot gusts of wind assaulted my face and chapped my skin. A sudden and overbearing thirst strangled my throat and choked me to the point of gagging.

It became harder and harder to breathe as I felt my eyes slowly roll back in my head. As soon as I felt myself ready to collapse, the exact opposite took place.

Suddenly my bones began to ache and I felt my teeth chater. My thirst was vanquished and I could now see my breath. My skin was now stung and red from the cold. The more I tried to warm myself, the colder I became.

I now found myself at the center of this realm which was in fact a large glacier. Within the perimiters of the glacier, the bitter wind shrilled as the snow cut through my skin. I was within extreme cold, within extreme heat. I was trapped in the most brutal blizzard at the center of Hell. At the top of this glacier sat a huge throne far too big for any mortal man. Even more peculiar was that the throne was made up of the debris of different world landmarks. Sitting in this destructively decorated throne was a giant who only revealed his silhouette to me.

Finally one last agony befell me;perhaps the greatest of all the pains I had endured thus far. I gained the full knowledge of what this place was, why I was needed and who exactly sat in front of me.

Before I could speak however the black robes appeared before me and removed their hoods and masks, confirming what I suspected to know. Their identities revealed were that of my own self in the past, present and future. Different stages of my life that had been lived and others that would follow.

The first robe was an angry youth. The second was a bitter man. The third was an elder that had gone mad. The fourth was a soul lost in despair. Each robe appeared more corrupt and tainted than the one before it.

I also soon discovered what the pendilum was that they had tried so hard to keep from showing me. It was a silver crucifix that was given to me at the time of my birth and that I had worn through the years and evidentaly for the rest of my life. However from the first black robe to the fourth, the crucifix became less illustrious and more tarnished due to the nature of my sins.

At the very height of this evil sat the being upon the throne of ruins . . . someone, something;surely I was not destined to become!? This abomination now fully shown to me. A giant in war worn armor that had been stained with the blood of countless lives. In it's mighty fist it clenched a huge barbaric sword that was coated with the phantasmic screams of butchered souls. Held aloft in it's other hand was an enormous, ungodly chalice that overflowed with the death of billions. Yet with all these macabre profanities, even more explicit to me was the fact that the crucifix was now no longer to be found; only the chain by which it was once held.

"Welcome to your kingdom" the giant spoke to me. "The fruits of your labor have been harvested here. Come, bask in it's splendor."

As much as it pained me, I found that the words somehow escaped my lips.

"It is true then, you and I . . ." "Indeed! We are one in the same;I am what you are destined to become. Tell me, younger self, do you know how all of this came to be?"

At first these revelations, these memories of the future, came to me slowly and in a hazy manner.

"In life, I fought for justice. Many times did I expose the wicked and crusade against evil. I longed to help the exploited and neglected. I gave alms. I prayed. I did all that I could to uphold God's law . . . to follow the path of the holy."

"How did the world react to your actions?" the giant enquired. As I began to recount these painful memories, they soon flooded my conscience with an unwavering force.

"No! It wasn't supposed to turn out this way!" I yelled as I realized the nature of my crimes.

"Answer me!" the giant demanded. "How did the world react?"

I felt an old but familiar hatred stirring up from the depths of my soul. It's seething nature sunk it's fangs into my being as I clenched my fists. Suddenly the various symbols on my body began to glow that dreadful color. "The world? The world was . . . IgNoRaNt and . . . UnGrAtEfUl. The world! The world . . . ShUnNeD me . . . and MoCkEd me."

"YeSsSsSsSsSsSs . . ." The giant spoke in a satisfied manner.

"No! NO! I just wanted to do what was right! I wanted to uphold honor. I wanted to save souls but . . ."

"The people cLuNg To ThEiR sIns"

I dropped to my knees in an overwhelming sense of defeat.

"Yes . . . I tried so hard. Few if any would listen. As the years passed more and more decadent behavior was being rewarded. Vices of every nature became commonplace. The people writhed in a constant dance of sacrilege and blasphemy. The battle I was fighting seemed to be in vain. In the end . . ."

"What of your final moments?"

"Why should I have bothered?? What difference did it make?? Let them ChOkE oN tHeIr OwN vOmIt! Let them DrOwN iN tHeIr OwN FiLtH! . . . NO! STOP IT! I refuse to believe this is how it all turns out!"

The giant laughed wildly, "Oh to be seduced by eViL! How could I ever resist the TeMpTaTiOn?? Who am I to deny InDuLgEnCe?? One of the greatest forms of eViL is that which had the potential to become RiGhTeOuS! In our final moments we made that last crucial decision. Do you remember now? Do YoU rEmEmBeR nOw??"

At that moment it felt as if all the pains and agonies of Hell rested upon my very being when the realization came full circle. "We . . . I . . . made a pact with evil in my final moments. I was so disgusted and embittered. I no longer wanted to save souls;I wanted to DaMn ThEm. I wanted to destroy a world so infatuated with . . . WiCkEdNeSs."

"And punish the ones who drove us to MaDnEsS!!"

"In seven days and seven nights I nearly obliterated the world with an unholy power. I no longer cared about good and evil; I just wanted to watch terror paint itself on all their PrOuD fAcEs! My path was one of endless slaughter. I took countless lives and then condemned their souls to my newfound kingdom at the end of purgatory and the begining of Hell. There I could bask in the joy of . . . PuNiShInG tHeM fOr EtErNiTy . . .

NOOOO! Damn you! Stay out of my mind! This isn't happening;this is all some illusion!"

"An illusion? What can you call an illusion in a glorious kingdom such as ours?? A kingdom that bends reality and warps time! A kingdom where good and evil bleed together in a portrait of unending mayhem. This kingdom of ours that prevented us from seeing the face of God, because wE cOuLd NoT fOrGiVe!!!"

With a combination of self-loathing and a desperate attempt for atonement, I arose to my feet and charged at the giant. As soon as I reached striking distance however, he grabbed me by the neck and threw me across the realm.

"**FOOL!** You cannot destroy me, we are one in the same. The pact has already been made! I summoned you here for the same reason that I called all the other versions of myself."

Dazed and having had the wind knocked out of me, my eyes slowly focused on the giant once more. When I tried to get up, an intense pain shot up my legs;they were broken and I could not move.

"During the course of eternity one runs out of sinners to damn and criminals to punish. Oh, how we believed this kingdom would grant us happiness! I tried every which way to achieve it! I qUaRtErEd them! I sKiNnEd them! bUrNeD them! sTrAnGlEd them! bUtChErEd them!

With every proclamation that the giant yelled, screams from all the other realms could be heard violently echoing to the center of this supernatural throneroom.

"Yet paradise could not be found in this kingdom. But then I realized what was missing! The one person who deserves to be honnored the most among all my subjects . . ."

"Me . . . and every other version of ourselves;every stage of our lives. We could not forgive others, and so we were not forgiven. That was the greatest sin of all to us, because it kept us from entering into Heaven."

"Yes! How I despise myself for those final weak moments. So much so, that I manipulated time to call all of us here. We, the greatest of evils must be punished and forsaken for all time. You are the last one I needed to bring forth in order to finish this act and make my kingdom complete! Come now! rEap your ReWaRdS! Take your RiGhTfUl place upon this ThRoNe!"

At once, the four black robes gathered around the giant and began levitating around him. They flew faster and faster in a vicious circle until all of their forms seemed to come together in one giant ball of light. The light was so brilliant that it blinded me and forced me to shut my eyes.

After a few moments, I regained my vision and beheld the most horrific monstrosity. The four robes and the giant had morphed together to form one great entity. A behemoth in fact, made up of the giant's head and a cluster of body parts from the robes. Various arms from the robes could be seen extending from the body of the behemoth and attacking the beast. The knife that one hand held was used to cut into it's flesh;while the other that held the chalice spilled acid on the mammoth. Still, one beat it with a club while the other whipped it's skin raw.

It was then that the giant's meaning truely took effect as I now understood the nature of this hell. That is, to punish and be punished. To torment and be tormented. To damn and be damned.

The mouths of the black robes danced along the body of the behemoth and screamed at me as they bit into the nightmarish creature. The giant's eye sockets cast pillars of fire and lightining. It's tounge resembling a great serpent made of blood and saltwater, spewing venom and speaking sacrilege in every language. It's feet like an elephant's trampled the ground and sent violent earthquakes throughout the realm.

At last the hellish beast regained a moment of sanity from it's own pain and approached me with only one thought in mind;to obliterate me, and itself completely.

This abomination of hatred and evil loomed over my battered body and lifted one of it's enormous legs over me. Slowly it began to lower it's gigantic foot downward with every intent to crush me like an insect.

Sweat poured from my brow;I felt so helpless. Was this the way it would all end? Not only for myself, but for all the souls condemned here. An eternity of physical and spiritual destruction. An unending death for all with no escape from it's relentless malice.

As the behemoth's foot was nearly upon me, an idea suddenly formed in my mind as if divinely inspired. If we truely were one in the same, then we would share all of our characteristics. Just as the giant revealed my future evil, perhaps I could remind him of my past good. Was it possible at all? Could there be any purity at all in the depths of this beast? I could only pray as I tried, for it was the very last chance for salvation.

I quickly tore the crucifix off of my neck and pushed it as hard as I could against the mammoth's foot. Suddenly light emitted from the crucifix and began to burn into the monster's skin. At once the beast raised it's leg and inspected it's foot. As it observed the crucifix the beast howled and wailed as I could feel it's mind reeling back so many years ago. It's mind flooded with acts of charity and kindness;it's heart overwhelmed with feelings of love and compassion. All of the aspects which had become so foreign and lost in it's overzealous quest; now radiated throughout this tormented devil.

Suddenly it's old, tired body was set aflame with a brilliant fire. A fire not of pain or punishment, but rather one of great renewel and purification. The flames became so spectacular, that it's light shown throughout the entire realm.

Then the holy flames began to consume the beast's body until only the image of an old man wrapped in light was left.

"Oh, thank you so much! I have waited for countless millenia in the hope that I might one day be freed from the prison that I had made. You see younger self, my rage was also bravado and lies. I did not summon different phases of myself to punish them, but rather in the hopes that they could set myself, and all the others free. For

I needed a version of myself that still knew what was good and could show me how to forgive. In my quest for justice, I forgot the very fundamentals of the side I fought for. All of my other selves failed to revert my being and so I condemnded them here with me. You were my last chance to atone for my great errors. I played a deadly game of judge, jury and executioner; and the world almost paid the ultimate price. Thank you younger self, at last I can be at peace and serve my God. He is the merciful One and I shall leave the matters of everyone else in His hands."

The old man raised his hand before me and sent out the four black robes before me. Suddenly the entire realm began to tremor and quake.

"Now you must leave this diminsion at once; for it was never meant to be! Make haste towards this hell's entrance;as you go through and leave the different realms, our acts of vice will be erased and the condemned will have their souls returned to their bodies. Their lives will be given back to them and history will be rewritten. But you must hurry, this peverse reality should never have been; it is now fading fast and will soon dissapear. If you cannot escape it then all time will be lost and the very fabric of reality destroyed. The black robes will take you;for they too must go back and be relieved of their burdens, until time only exisits at your point in life and proper balance restored. Farewell."

The old man wrapped in light floated towards the heavens and became transparent until he dissapeared completely. Just then, the four black robes circled around me and with their combined power began to levitate me off of the ground. They quickly carried me out of the realm of "**GRUDGE**." As they did my mind began to see catastrophes of the world being erased from time;tragidies that I had brought on vanished completely.

Then we pased through the realm of "**DEATH**" and I saw all of the souls of these condmened being released. The many different souls flew off into various directions until they escaped the realm. I could now see in my mind lives being carried out and ending the way they were destined to;my interference was taken away. The blood returned to their veins and was no longer on my soul. Just as we were about to leave, the black robe of this realm dissapeared. That aspect of my life was erased from time.

The same things occured as we passed through the other realms of "**SELF**", "**PROFIT**" and "**MOCKERY**". My evil deeds of the future were no more, and countless lives and souls were restored. To my suprise I was given more insight to the way that many of the formerly condemned would eventually live their lives. Although many did do terrible and hurtful things in their lives;there were also an abundant number who changed with time and made amends . . . something that they would not have been able to do had their lives been taken prematurely.

The third and the second black robes also vanished as did my sins. The realms were dissapearing into oblivion and soon this would all be as just some horrible nightmare that would be forgotten.

Only one robe now remained and struggled to use what little power there was left to carry me to the entrance. We were now at the very begining in the maze of curtains. The entrance was now only a stone's throw away, when all of a sudden the robe vanished and I dropped to the floor. All of my crimes were now no more, and all would be right with the world. But I still needed to go through the entrance to make it all so. As I began to crawl towards the doorway, I winced at the terrible pain that shot through my legs.

I mustered every ounce of strength that I had to make it through.

—Please God, if I could just pass—my mind begged.

Then as my fingertips stretched through the doorway; everything turned white. My whole body went numb and there was no sense of anything.

Was I too late? Is this it? Is this . . . nothingness?

"STEP RIGHT UP AND TEST YOUR STRENGTH! WIN A PRIZE FOR YOUR GIRLFRIEND!"

I jerked my head up at the loud noise and saw that I was sitting on a bench in the middle of the carnival. The many different lights were brightly shining;the music was blaring and the hustle and bustle of people was all about. I looked around to survey the area and found no sign of the haunted house. In it's place was a large merry-go-round with many children riding it and playing about. Their laughter was surely welcome, but had I just been asleep the whole time? Was this just some strange dream?

As I slowly arose from the bench, I felt a slight warmth against my chest. I looked down my shirt and was suprised when I saw the crucifix around my neck. It was now solid gold and shined more radiantly then it ever had!

So it was all true then;the ordeal of the black robes . . . But now fate was set back on it's proper tracks and all was at peace. I smiled as I left the carnival and headed for home. I knew that my future was going to be a bright one, and that an even greater reward would lie beyond.

AUTHOR BIOGRAPHY

Having grown up with obsessive-compulsive disorder and depression I chose creative writing as an outlet for my daily trials. In my teenage years I created many short stories in poetic verse, mostly of a dark nature, as a form of expression.

As I grew from a teenager to a young adult I recieved more recongnition of my work. However as my talents evolved so too did my symptoms progress. At one point in my life I was completely lost in despair and became very suicidal. After getting the help that I needed from many wonderful people including my loving family, I realized that many of the things I sought after were trivial at best.

I returned to the Catholic faith and began to concern myself with much more important matters that are disregarded by this world. I am now blessed with a peace and happiness that many do not know.

I live in the small town of Alton, Illinois where I take care of my father and continue to do holy hours at the adoration chapel in St. Anthony's hospital. I am an avid rpg video gamer and enjoy watching animation. I am also an animal lover and a huge fan of man's best friend.